Franklin Helps Out

From an episode of the animated TV series *Franklin* produced by Nelvana Limited, Neurones France s.a.r.l. and Neurones Luxembourg S.A.

Based on the *Franklin* books by Paulette Bourgeois and Brenda Clark.

TV tie-in adaptation written by Paulette Bourgeois and illustrated by Sean Jeffrey, Mark Koren and Jelena Sisic.

Based on the TV episode, *Franklin's Nature Hike*, written by Nicola Barton.

Franklin

Kids Can Press acknowledges the support of the Ontario Arts Council, the Canada Council for the Arts and the Government of Canada, through the BPIDP, for our publishing activity.

Kids Can Press Ltd.
29 Birch Avenue
Toronto, Ontario, Canada
M4V 1E2

Edited by Tara Walker
Designed by Karen Powers

Printed in Hong Kong by Wing King Tong Company Limited
This book is limp sewn with a drawn-on cover

CDN PA 00 0 9 8 7 6 5 4 3 2 1

Canadian Cataloguing in Publication Data

Main entry under title:

Franklin helps out

(A Franklin TV storybook)
Based on characters created by Paulette Bourgeois and Brenda Clark.

ISBN 1-55074-823-8 (bound)   ISBN 1-55074-825-4 (pbk.)

I. Bourgeois, Paulette. II. Clark, Brenda. III. Series: Franklin TV storybook.

PS8550.F725 2000   jC813'.54   C00-930982-9
PZ7.Fra 2000

Kids Can Press is a Nelvana company

Franklin Helps Out

Based on characters created by
Paulette Bourgeois and Brenda Clark

Kids Can Press

FRANKLIN could count by twos and tie his shoes. He liked to help Mr. Owl in the classroom, and he always lent a hand to friends and neighbours. But one day, Franklin was a little *too* helpful.

Franklin's class was going on a nature hike. Mr. Owl asked everyone to bring back something for the school nature display.

He reminded the students to leave living things in the woods, where they belonged.

Then he pointed out where Franklin and his friends might find some interesting nature objects.

Franklin could hardly wait to collect something
special.

"Let's go this way," he said to Snail.

But Snail didn't hear because he was too busy
looking at fungus.

Then, without asking, Franklin scooped up Snail.

"I'll give you a ride," said Franklin.

Snail was startled. He hadn't finished exploring yet.

Minutes later, Franklin spotted some milkweed. He
put Snail down and blew on the pods. The seeds floated
in the breeze.

"That looks like fun," thought Snail. He found a
whole pod of seeds for himself, but when he huffed
and puffed, nothing budged.

So Snail searched until he found a pod with one
small seed. He was about to blow on it when Franklin
picked him up.

"We're on our way," said Franklin. "I'll give you a
hand, Snail."

Snail sighed. He had wanted to blow on a seed, too.

There were lots of wonderful things to collect in the woods.

Beaver stuffed her backpack with pine cones, leaves and rocks.

"How many things do you have?" she asked Snail.

"None so far," answered Snail. "I'm waiting to find something really special."

After lunch, Bear discovered a wasps' nest.

"Wasps sting if you bother them," warned Beaver.

But Bear insisted the nest was empty.

Franklin set Snail near a log and took a closer look.
Then he heard a buzzing sound. "Oh no," he cried.

A cloud of angry wasps flew out.

"Run!" shouted Fox.

Franklin and his friends ran screaming down
the path.

"That was close," panted Beaver.
"That's the fastest I've ever run," said Goose.
"Me, too," said Franklin. "How about you, Snail?"
But Snail wasn't there to answer.

Franklin suddenly remembered that he'd left
Snail behind.

"Maybe the wasps stung Snail!" cried Franklin.
"I should have taken him with me."

Franklin and his friends raced back to the nest.
There was no sign of the wasps and no sign of Snail.

"Snail?" called Franklin. "Snail? Where are you?"

Snail had no idea that his friends were worried about him. He was busy exploring a network of termite tunnels.

Snail was puzzled when he heard Franklin's frantic calls.

"Here I am," said Snail, as he crawled out of the log.

Franklin rushed towards him. "Are you all right?"

"Of course," giggled Snail.

Everyone was relieved to see that Snail was safe.

Snail didn't understand all the fuss. "I'm fine," he said. "But I need to collect something."

"I'll help you," said Franklin, stooping to pick up his little friend.

"I can do it myself," said Snail.

But Franklin insisted.

Snail's head drooped and he let out a big sigh.

Franklin made sure he helped Snail all afternoon.

When Franklin found seeds, he put them into Snail's bag.

When he found beautiful pebbles, he kept one for himself and gave the other to Snail.

He even picked a leaf for Snail, although Snail could have done it by himself.

Franklin collected so many things that Snail could barely move.

When it was almost time to go back to school,
Snail still hadn't collected anything that *he* wanted.
Franklin offered to find something else.

Snail was annoyed. "I want to find my own special
things," he said firmly. Then he set off alone.

Franklin was hurt and puzzled.

"I just wanted to help," he told his friends. "Snail is small, and he doesn't move very fast."

"But he's good at doing things for himself," said Beaver. "In his own way."

Rabbit pointed to the cliff. Snail was climbing straight up the side.

"I told you," said Beaver.

"Wow," said Franklin. "It looks like Snail doesn't always need my help."

Soon, Snail slid down the cliff and showed his friends a sparkling quartz crystal.

Everyone oohed and aahed.

"That's the best find yet," said Franklin.

Snail smiled proudly.

Just then, Mr. Owl's whistle blew. "Better hurry back," said Beaver.

Franklin started to pick up Snail, but then he stopped.

"Can I give you a ride, Snail?" he asked.

"Sure," said Snail cheerfully. "I like getting help when I really need it."

Franklin ran so fast that some pebbles and leaves fell out of his bag.

"Don't worry," said Snail. "You can have one of my crystals."

"Thanks!" said Franklin.

Snail smiled. "I'm glad I could help."